Small Budget, Big Dreams

"Growing Up with Money: First Step to Financial Freedom"

Abdoulaye Amie Soumah, MBA

Abdoulaye Amie Soumah, MBA

Dedication

I dedicate this book to my children, and to every child and young dreamer around the world.

May you grow with the wisdom to understand that money is not merely something to spend, but a powerful tool to build, create, and serve. May you learn early the lessons that many generations discovered too late: the value of discipline, the dignity of honest work, and the importance of managing what you earn.

This book is also dedicated to parents who work tirelessly every day to give their children a better future. Your sacrifices, your hopes, and your love are the foundation upon which strong families and strong societies are built.

If these pages help even one young person understand that a small budget can still carry great dreams, then this work will have fulfilled its purpose.

May knowledge replace fear, may discipline replace confusion, and may every child grow with the confidence to build a life of dignity, responsibility, and financial freedom.

Abdoulaye Amie Soumah, MBA

My Why

The only reason I wrote this book is to serve the world.

Across the globe, millions of schools educate billions of students. People spend decades in classrooms, earn valuable diplomas, and accumulate knowledge in many fields. Yet, one essential subject is often missing: understanding money.

How can we build a better world if generations graduate without learning how to manage resources, create value, or build financial stability?

If we are truly committed to a better future, we must invest in the quality of human beings. We must equip people with the knowledge, discipline, and mindset that allow them not only to survive, but to thrive — to create value, take responsibility for their lives, and achieve financial independence.

The reality is simple: most schools do not teach financial literacy. But every great change begins with a decision.

This book is an invitation to change that paradigm — starting now.

Acknowledgment

First of all, I give thanks to my large family, the foundation of my stability and a permanent source of inspiration.

To my wife, **Mrs. Soumah**, a lifelong pillar, I pay a sincere and deeply deserved tribute for her unwavering support.

To my children, my brothers and sisters, and Mrs. Soumah's namesake club — the great Hawa — thank you for your attentive presence, affection, and constant encouragement.

Great leaders are not always the ones who give answers. Often, they are the ones who know how to ask the right questions — the ones that raise awareness and trigger action.

It is in this spirit that I would like to express my deep gratitude to **Mrs. Hawa Barry Diallo**, whom I affectionately and proudly call *my sister*. Through the simplicity and accuracy of a single question, she sowed in me a reflection which, over time, gave birth to this book, at the service of our community:

"Brother, our community needs to be educated about finances. Don't you think we can do something?"

This question, asked with sincerity and a sense of responsibility, was an act of authentic leadership. My sister, thank you for your vision, your commitment, and your ability to inspire action through reflection.

I also want to thank all those who deeply believe that a child who reads, learns and dreams can change the world. This book is for you.

Thank you to the parents, teachers and educators who accompany the young people in the discovery of the value of money, a job well done and responsibility.

Thank you to the **EduWealth Foundation** team, young readers and school clubs committed to this essential mission: to make knowledge a lever for freedom, dignity and hope.

Finally, thank you to all the children who will read this book. Remember: your dreams have infinite value, even if your budget is small. Your courage, curiosity and discipline will make you the builders of a better world.

Preface

This book was born from a dream: to make financial education accessible to all, from a young age.

Because understanding money also means understanding life, discipline and freedom.

Through these pages, each reader will discover that they don't need a big budget to have big dreams.

This book will guide you step by step to learn how to manage your money, save, dream and act wisely.

Little by little, you will understand that financial education is not a matter for rich adults, but a human adventure accessible to all.

Welcome to this journey of knowledge and financial responsibility.

Abdoulaye Amie Soumah, MBA

Message to the Reader

Dear friend,

If you hold this book in your hands, it's because you believe in yourself, in your future, and in the possibility of making your dreams come true. And you're right.

Because a dream only becomes reality when you learn to use what you have wisely.

This book is not a simple manual. It's a compass — a loyal friend that will accompany you on the path to financial freedom and selfconfidence.

You will discover how to manage your money, save intelligently, understand the true value of things, and above all, dream with strategy and courage.

In each chapter, you'll find stories, activities, and challenges to help you think, understand, and act.

Read at your own pace. Take notes. Talk to your family or friends. Share your discoveries.

Remember:

Money is just a tool, but knowledge is your true power.

A key to changing your future

Stop for a moment and think:

Small Budget, Big Dreams

How many adults around you work hard, day in and day out, without ever really being free?

Why do so many families remain prisoners of lack, generation after generation?

Why do some parents never have enough time for their children?

Why do so many people live exhausted, without peace, despite all their efforts?

The answer is simple:

They were taught to make money, but not to understand it. They were taught to work, but not to become free.

They have been taught to spend, but rarely to invest. You hold a precious key in your hands.

A key that will help you understand that even with a small budget, you can build big dreams.

A key to learning what many discover too late:

- That money should serve you, not direct you.
- Let true wealth begin in your mind before it is seen in your pocket.
- Let every great journey begin with a small step, but in the right direction.

This book is more than a guide:

It's a call.

A call to dare to think differently, to break routine, to refuse the fate of lack and to choose the path of freedom.

Every page you read is a weapon against financial ignorance.

Every idea you understand is a seed for your future.

So... Are you ready to change your story?

If so, take a deep breath... and turn the page.

Your journey to freedom starts here.

Objective of the Book

Introduce children and their families to the basics of financial education in a simple, pictorial and motivating way, to sow the seeds of financial independence early.

Table of Contents

Introduction

Have you ever heard that money grows on trees? Of course not! Yet, money is something that everyone uses every day: to eat, to go to school, to travel, or to make their dreams come true. But do you know one thing? Most children and even many adults don't really understand how money works. As a result, they work very hard but don't always feel free or happy with what they earn.

That's why this little book was written. It is for you, for your brothers and sisters, and also for your parents. It will teach you the basics of financial education with simple words and easy-to-understand examples. You will discover concepts such as:

- What is a budget?
- What is the difference between an asset and a liability?
- How can you tell the difference between spending and investment?
- Why is it important to save and have a plan for your dreams?

But most importantly, this book will show you that even if you start with a small budget, you can have big dreams and achieve them if you learn how to manage your money well.

To Parents: This book is also for you. It will give you tools to talk about money with your children so that they grow up with the right mentality and avoid the costly mistakes of adult life.

So, get ready to embark on a great adventure. An adventure where money is no longer a mystery but a tool to build your future. Welcome to the world of financial education!

CHAPTER 1: Why Talk About Money at a Young Age?

Managing Your Money from a Young Age

Chapter 1
Why talk about money at a young age?

Have you ever seen an adult stressed about money? Maybe your parents sometimes talk about bills, groceries, or rent. However, at school, you were never taught how money works. Weird, right?

Many people grow up without understanding the rules of money. The result? They become adults, work hard, but never manage to be financially free.

Why? Because they have never learned how money is earned, kept, and worked. This means that there is a good chance that they will not be able to pursue their passions or truly do what they love in life.

Talking about money in the family is not a taboo. On the contrary, the more you understand how money works, the better choices you can make in your life.

Want to help your family? Start by learning how to manage your own money.

Do you want to be free later? Start by learning how to make your money work, instead of just working for it. You don't have to be an adult to understand these things. You can start today.

Small Challenge: Ask a parent how he or she learned to manage money. Write down his/her answer in your learning notebook.

Managing your money from a young age

The History of Yarie and Her Golden Coins

Yarie was ten years old and loved sweet patties. Every Sunday, her father gave her 5,000 Guinean francs as pocket money. But on Monday, the little girl would run to the neighborhood shop to buy sweets and cookies. By Friday, she had nothing left, and when her best friends Binta, Fanta, and Sia wanted to go to the school cinema, Yarie would say sadly:
"I have no more money."

One day, her grandmother, a wise woman from the village, said to her gently:

"My daughter, your money is like a bird. If you open your hand without thinking, it flies away. But if you teach it to build a little nest, it will always come back with friends."

Intrigued, Yarie asked:

"And how do we build this nest, grandmother?"

"By keeping a little of what we receive, each time."

So, the following week, Yarie decided to change. Of her 5,000 francs, she put 1,000 in a small empty box that she called "My Dream Box." The other 4,000 were still used to buy some sweets, but now she had one goal: to save a little for later.

After a few weeks, the box was filled with coins. She was so proud that she ran to show her treasure to her grandmother. "Bravo, Yarie! You've learned the first rule: it's not the quantity that counts, but the habit of keeping a little of what you earn."

And that day, Yarie understood something important: managing your money is about respecting yourself.

Financial Tip

Even a small amount can become a big one if you save it regularly.

Try to keep 10% of everything you receive, even if it's only 100 francs.

Reflection

Have you ever thought about what you could achieve if you kept a little money every week?

A book? A pencil case? Or even your first small project?

Challenge

1. Find a special box or envelope and name it "My Dream."
2. Every week, put a little money into it, even if it's just a small coin.
3. In a month, look at how much you've saved!

CHAPTER 2: What exactly is money?

Money is a tool
Money has no emotion
What is the money used for?

Chapter 2
What Exactly Is Money?

You hear about money every day. But do you really know what it is? Before the notes and coins we use today, people exchanged things. We called it bartering.

For example:

- "I'll give you a fish."
- "And you give me rice."

But it wasn't always practical. So humans invented money.

Money Is a Tool

Money is used to buy, exchange, save, invest, and give. It's a bit like a Swiss Army knife: you can use it in many ways, but you have to learn how to handle it.

Imagine that you have 1,000 francs. You can:

- Buy a candy
- Keep that money in a box
- Give it to a friend
- Make it multiply by buying something that you will sell for more

Money Has No Emotion

Some people say, "Money is bad." But money has no emotion. It doesn't make people mean or nice. It's how you use it that counts.

A generous person can use money to help others. A miserly person can keep everything to himself. Money reveals what you are.

Gambling: What Is Money Used For?

Here's a little activity.

Connect every word to the right action:

Word	Action
1. Buy	a) Save some of the money for later
2. Save	b) Helping a person in difficulty
3. Donate	c) Buy a book or food

Answers:
1 → c, 2 → a, 3 → b

To Remember:

- Money is not bad; it is a tool.
- It can help you achieve your dreams if you learn how to use it well.
- You can start to better understand its role today.

Small Challenge:

Draw a coin or a note and write down what you would like to do with it:

- One thing for you
- One thing for others
- One thing for your future

The Importance of Saving

The Story of Soulemane and His Wooden Car

Soulemane loved to make toys. With pieces of wood, he built small cars that he proudly drove in the courtyard. But one day, he saw a beautiful red remote-controlled car in a shop window. It shone, advanced, retreated, and turned by itself!

He fell in love with it.

"Dad, I want this car!" he cried enthusiastically.

"Agreed," replied his father, "but it costs 80,000 francs. And you know, I can't buy everything at once. If you really want that car, let's save together."

Soulemane thought. He had some money received at a party: 20,000 francs.

His father proposed an idea:

"Every week, you keep a little of what you receive, and I'll do the same. When your piggy bank is full, we'll see where you are."

Small Budget, Big Dreams

This is how Soulemane began to save seriously. While his friends spent everything at the kiosk on chips or juices, he carefully put 2,000 francs in his box each time. The first few weeks, it wasn't easy. Sometimes he wanted to spend it all. But he remembered his red car, and he resisted.

Three months later, he opened his box with a big smile: he had reached 50,000 francs!

His father, proud of him, added the rest. Together, they went to buy the car they had dreamed of.

That day, Soulemane understood one essential thing: Saving is the patience that turns small efforts into big wins.

Fanta's Story and Her Dream of a Bicycle

Fanta lived a few kilometers from her school. Every morning, she set off on foot with her schoolbag on her back, crossing the dusty paths of the village. She often dreamed of having a blue bicycle, like her cousin Aliko's. "One day, I'll go to school by bike too," she said to herself every morning.

But this dream seemed big. Her parents couldn't afford to buy one right away.

One day, during a workshop at school, the teacher explained:

- "Big dreams often start with a small plan. If you want something, write it down, put it in numbers, and take action every day to get closer to it."

Fanta took this sentence very seriously. That same evening, she took a notebook and wrote:

- My dream: to buy a blue bicycle.
- Estimated price: 300,000 francs.
- Duration: 6 months.

She then decided to do a small business: selling colorful bracelets that she made with beads given to her aunt. Every day after school, she made two or three, which she sold to her classmates. Every franc she earned went into a small box that she proudly called "My Bike Project."

Six months later, Fanta walked into the neighborhood store, her notebook and box in her hand. She put her savings on the counter, her heart pounding.

That day, she went home on her blue bicycle, smiling bigger than the sky. She then understood that dreams only become reality when they are transformed into concrete plans.

Financial Tip

When you receive money, think first of what you want to build, not what you want to consume. Every piece you set aside is a seed for your future.

A dream becomes closer when you turn it into a project.

Write down your goal, set an amount, and set a timeline. That's what planning for success is all about.

Small Budget, Big Dreams

Reflection

Why do you think some people achieve their dreams faster than others?

Because they have learned to wait for the right moment and to prepare for their successes.

What are the three dreams you would like to achieve this year?
And above all, what can you start doing today to get closer to them?

Challenge:

1.   Write down a dream that you would like to fulfill by the end of the year.
2.   Calculate how much you need to get there.
3.   Decide how much you can save each week to get closer.
4.   Choose a concrete dream (book, uniform, bike, tablet...).
5.   Write down its price and how many weeks it would take you to save.
6.   Create your own "dream plan" in a notebook or on a piece of paper to display in your room.

CHAPTER 3: Need or want? Learn to make a difference!

Why is this important?

Chapter 3
Need or Want? Learn to Make a Difference!

Why Is This Important?

Imagine you're at the market with your mom. You see a beautiful toy. You absolutely want to have it! But your mom tells you:

- "Today, we came to buy rice, not a toy."

You're a little disappointed... But do you know why she said no? Because she chose a need instead of a desire.

What's the Difference?

A need is something essential to live.

Without it, you're in danger or you can't grow well.

Examples:

- Food
- Water
- Clothing to protect yourself
- Going to school
- Treating yourself in case of illness

A desire is something that we like to have, but which is not essential.

Examples:

- An ice cream
- A new game
- A state-of-the-art phone
- Fashionable sneakers
- Eating at fast food restaurants

Why Is This Important?

Because money is not infinite! If we spend everything on wants, we won't have enough for needs.

An intelligent child learns to make a difference and prioritize.

Tip: The Three-Question Rule

When you want to buy something, ask yourself these three questions:

1. Do I really need it to live or learn?
2. Can I wait a little longer before getting it?
3. Do I already have something that does the same thing?

If you answer "yes" to all three, it's probably a desire.

Little Exercise: Need or Want?

Read the sentences below. Next to each object, write "N" if it's a need and "D" if it's a desire.

1. A notebook for school: ____
2. A new game console: ____

3. Medications: ___
4. A pizza for a snack: ___
5. A bottle of water: ___
6. Candy: ___

Answers:
1-N, 2-D, 3-N, 4-D, 5-N, 6-D

To Remember:

- Needs are mandatory; desires are optional.
- Knowing how to make a difference means being smart with money.
- When you prioritize needs, you show that you are responsible.

Small Challenge:

For a week, write down everything you want to buy. In the end, separate what is a need and what is a desire.

CHAPTER 4: Your first budget

What is a budget?
Why is this important?
How do I create a small budget?

Chapter 4
Your First Budget

Imagine that you receive 50,000 francs every week as pocket money. What do you do with it?

Do you spend it all in one day? Saving some money? Are you giving something to a friend?

You have just made, without knowing it, your very first budget.

What is a budget?

A budget is simply a plan.

It tells you:

- How much do you have
- What do you want to do with it
- And how not to waste it all

When you make a budget, you decide in advance how to use your money wisely.

Why is this important?

Because without a budget, you will face these:

- Spending more than you have
- Don't save anything for later
- Not knowing where your money has gone

But with a budget:

- You are in control of your money
- You can achieve your goals (like buying a book or a bicycle)
- You feel less stress

How do I create a small budget?

Here is a simple method with 30,000 francs:

Usage	Recommended percentage	Amount for 30,000
Useful expenses (snacks, transport, etc.)	50 %	15.000
Savings (for a project or an emergency)	30 %	9.000
Giving/sharing (family, friends, almsgiving)	10 %	3.000
Hobbies (movies, sweets)	10 %	3.000

Game: Your Personalized Budget

Try filling in your own table:

I received _________ F this week.

What do I want to do with it?

Usage	Amount
Useful expenditure	
Savings	
Donation / Sharing	
Leisure	

Tip: If you want to save for a project, write it next to "Save". Example: "To buy a book in a month."

To remember:

- The budget is a control tool: it helps you keep power over your money.
- It shows you that there is a time for everything: spending, saving, giving, having fun.
- A good budget = a better organized life.

Small challenge: Create a budget for the next two weeks. Ask an adult to check it with you.

CHAPTER 5: Active or Passive? (The Super Power of the Clever Children)

What is an asset?
Examples of assets
What is a liability?
Little magic board

Chapter 5
Assets or Liabilities? (The Super Power of the Clever Children)

Imagine two children:

- Agnès buys a toy. She plays for a few days... Then crack, it breaks and disappears from her life.
- Bamory buys a small oven. He makes biscuits, sells them, earns money, and ends up buying a bike!

Which child made the best choice?

Bamory! Because he bought... an asset.

This word can change your whole life. So come on, I'll explain.

1. What is an asset?

An asset is something that makes you money or that retains its value over a long time.

It's like a magic plant: you water it once, and it gives you coins every week.

Examples of asset ingredients:

- A piggy bank full of savings
- A book that you can reread and that teaches you something
- A bike that allows you to deliver bread
- A tool to sell cookies or make something
- A computer to learn to code

Asset works for you, even when you're sleeping!

2. What are liabilities?

A liability is something that takes your money and quickly loses its value.

It's like a balloon bursting after a day: you're happy at first, then... nothing.

Examples of liabilities:

- A fragile toy that breaks quickly
- Candies that you finish in 2 minutes
- Very expensive shoes that you almost never wear
- A state-of-the-art phone... Just to play

A liability makes you happy now, but it doesn't bring you anything afterwards.

3. Little Magic Board

Purpose	Asset or Liability?	Why?
A piggy bank	Asset	It keeps your money
A fragile toy	Liability	It breaks fast
An educational book	Asset	You learn again, and again
Sweets	Liability	They disappear in a few minutes
A small candy shop	Asset	It makes you money

4. Test: Guess the Asset!

1   A bicycle to deliver bread: __

2   Designer shoes you wear once: ___

3   A computer to learn to code: ____

Answers: 1-Asset, 2-Liability, 3-Asset

5.   What the rich understand

Rich people think like this:

First, I buy assets.

With the money my assets generate, I can treat myself.

The poor, on the other hand, mainly buy liabilities that disappear quickly.

You can choose to be in the first category... right now.

6.   How do you know if something is an asset or a liability?

Ask yourself one magic question:

"Will it pay off... or cost me?"

- If it puts money in your pocket→ Asset
- If it takes money out of your pocket→ Liability

Simple, but powerful.

7.   Small challenge for you

Challenge 1:

Look at your room and make 2 lists:

- List A: Items that help you earn or save money
- List B: Items you like but don't earn anything

Challenge 2:

Find 3 small assets that you could create or obtain in the next 6 months.

Talk to an adult to help you get started.

Exercise:

Look at the images below and describe the objects as an asset. or a liability?

According to you, Aicha and Moussa, who is on the path to financial freedom

Use these lines to make your list

1) Assets

....

....

....

....

2) Liabilities

....

....

....

CHAPTER 6: Passive Income — The Secret to Financial Freedom

Active vs. Passive Income
Why Passive Income Is "Magic"
How to Create Passive Income

Chapter 6
Passive Income — The Secret to Financial Freedom

Imagine that you continue to earn money while you're sleeping, playing, or spending time with your family.

This is called **passive income**.

Unlike **active income**, it does not depend directly on the time you spend working.

It's a powerful idea: **make money work for you**, instead of always working for money.

Active vs. Passive Income

- **Active income**: You trade your time for money. If you stop working, the money stops too.

Example: a teacher, a driver, a doctor, or a shopkeeper earns money only when he/she works.

- **Passive income**: You put in the effort at first, and then your money or idea continues to generate income even when you're no longer working directly.

Example: a book sold online, a rented house, stocks that pay dividends, or an app you created that people use.

Why Passive Income Is "Magic"

This type of income is magical because it **frees up your time.**

It allows you to spend more time with your family, pursue your passions, or even help others, while still receiving money.

It's a key to **financial freedom**: you no longer need to depend on a single job to live.

But be careful! It's not instant magic.

We must first learn**, prepare, and build** this system.

Passive income rewards **those who think long-term.**

How to Create Passive Income (Even Starting Small)

1. **Learn and discover your talents**.

Look for what you know how to do naturally: writing, drawing, teaching, coding, making, singing...

Every talent can become a source of ideas.

2. **Create something useful**.

Passive income is born from smart work:

- write a book or create an e-book,
- design an educational game,
- produce a useful YouTube video,
- create a small online business.
- create a comic book and sell it to the school

- Make personalized bracelets and sell them with your name on them
- record an audio story and propose it to other children

3.   **Invest wisely**.

Even with a small budget, you can start saving for an asset: something that will pay off in the future.

It can be a machine, a tool, a course, or an idea you're developing.

4.   **Be patient**.

Passive income doesn't grow overnight. You have to **nurture your idea, improve it, and make it known**.

Over time, the results appear.

Inspiring example

Think of an author writing an educational book. He spent weeks writing, correcting, and publishing it. But once the book is online, it continues to sell every month, even while the author is doing something else.

Each sale is a reward for his initial work.

This is the power of passive income

"Passive income is not magic. It is the reward of knowledge, perseverance, and creativity.

You don't have to be rich to get started. You just have to believe that you can learn and build. »

At the beginning, you work once... But after that, the money can continue to come; it works for you.

Game: True or false?

1. Passive income falls from the sky. ___
2. It sometimes takes a lot of work at the beginning. ___

3. A passbook that is sold every week is passive income. ___
4. If I sleep, the money can still come in because of a good system. ___

Answers: 1-False, 2-True, 3-True, 4-True

To remember:

• Passive income is like a seed that you plant to harvest later.
• It makes you freer because you don't trade your time for money.
• Even as a child, you can start small, with a simple idea.

Small challenge: Imagine a project that you can do once, and that can pay off many times over. Write it down, draw it, or discuss it with an adult!

CHAPTER 7:
Understanding the Stock Market

What is the stock market?
Why do people buy stocks?
How does the market work?
Why learn the stock market early?
Inspirational citation

Chapter 7
Understanding the Stock Market

Imagine you own a small sandwich restaurant. Customers love your products, and you want to open more stores. But you don't have enough money to finance everything yourself. You then decide to **sell shares in your company** to people who believe in your project.

These people become **the owners of a part of your company**: they are **the shareholders**.

What is the stock market?

The stock market is the place (physical or online) where people buy and sell small portions of companies, which are called shares.

It's a bit like a big market, but instead of selling rice, fish, or clothes, they sell pieces of companies!

Large companies such as Apple, Coca-Cola, Orange, and Total are listed on stock exchanges. This means that anyone [you (with the help of parents), your parents, your teachers...] can buy a very small part of them.

Why do people buy stocks? There are two main reasons:

1. To make money when the value of the stock increases.

For example, you buy a stock at $10, and a few months later, it's worth $15. You win $5.

2. To receive dividends means a portion of the profits that the company distributes to its shareholders.

But be careful! Stocks can also lose value. That's why you have to learn, observe, and be patient before investing.

How does the market work?

The Exchange brings together:

- Companies (which need money to grow),
- Investors (who want to grow their money),
- And trading platforms (the intermediaries that facilitate transactions).

Every day, the price of shares rises and falls according to:

- the performance of the company,
- the country's economy,
- news around the world,
- and investor confidence.

It's a bit like the waves of the sea: sometimes calm, sometimes choppy. You have to know how to surf intelligently.

Why learn the stock market early?

Because the **younger you start, the earlier you understand how money works.**

Investing is not about playing at random; it is about **understanding companies, analysing their projects, and believing in their future**.

You don't have to be rich to be interested in the stock market.

What is needed is **curiosity, discipline, and the courage to learn.**

We can summarize that:

- The stock market is where companies' shares are bought and sold.
- Actions make it possible **to participate in the success of companies.**
- There are risks, but also **great opportunities** if you learn how to invest well.
- Learning about the stock market means **learning to grow your money** rather than letting it sit in savings and lose value due to inflation.

Mini-educational activity: "If I were an investor..."

1. Choose three companies that you know well (e.g., Apple, Nike, Orange, MTN, Canal+...)

2. For each, answer these three questions:

. What does this company sell?

. Why do people love its products?

. If I had money, would I like to buy a small share (a share)? Why?

3. Share your thoughts with a relative, friend, or teacher.

You'll see that **understanding a company is already thinking like an investor. Inspirational citation:**

"Don't just work for money, make your money work for you." — Robert Kiyosaki

Important words to remember

Share: a part of ownership in a company

Dividend: a portion of the profit you receive

Stock market: place where shares are bought and sold

Investing: Using your money to pay off later

Risk: possibility of losing money too **Game: True or False?**

1. Buying a share is like owning a small piece of a company. __
2. You are sure to always win when you invest. __
3. Children can never learn about the stock market. __

4. A company that is doing well can make your actions more valuable. __

Answers: 1-True, 2-False, 3-False, 4-True **To remember:**
- A share is a small part of a company.

- The stock exchange is a place where you buy and sell these stocks.
- *You can make or lose money, so you have to learn before you act.*

Small challenge: Choose a company you like (e.g., Orange, MTN, Coca-Cola, etc.) and find out if it's on the stock market. Imagine that you have a share in this company. What would you do to make it even more successful?

CHAPTER 8: Saving, Your Faithful Friend

What is savings?
Where to keep your savings?
Why is it important to save young?
Game: Your Savings Goal

Chapter 8

Saving as Your Loyal Friend

Have you ever heard this proverb? "Little by little, the bird makes its nest."

That's exactly what saving does!

It's the habit of setting aside some of your money for later. Even if it's a little, over time, it becomes a lot.

What are savings?

Saving is when you receive money (pocket money, gifts, rewards, etc.) and don't spend it all.

You keep a part for:

- A future project
- An emergency
- Or even a dream (travel, bike, book...)

It's your loyal friend because it saves you when you need it!

Where to keep your savings?

Here are some ideas:

- A piggy bank or secure box
- A savings account at the bank (with the help of an adult)
- A notebook to keep track of how much you keep each week

Why is it important to save young?

Because:

- You learn to be responsible
- You're prepared for the unexpected
- You can carry out your projects without always asking others

And above all... You get into a **_good habit_** for your future life.

Simple example

Imagine that you save 2,000 GNF every week.

Week	Amount saved
1	2,000 GNF
2	4,000 GNF
3	6,000 GNF
4	8,000 GNF

In a month, you already have 8,000 GNF without realizing it!

What if you continue? In six months, you can reach 48,000 GNF!

Game: Your Savings Goal

1. What is your project or your dream? ______
2. How much does it cost? ____________
3. How much can you save each week? _____
4. How long will it take you to get it? ________

Share your savings plan with an adult and ask them to help you stay motivated.

To remember:

- Saving means thinking about tomorrow.
- It's not what you earn that counts, but what you keep.
- The earlier you save, the stronger and freer you are later.

Small challenge: Start today! Take a box or envelope. Write your first name and your goal on it. Every week, put a little money into it. You'll be proud of yourself!

CHAPTER 9: Making Money When You're Young? Yes, it is possible!

Why make money young?
Simple ideas for children and teenagers
What to always remember

Chapter 9
Making Money When You're Young? Yes, it is possible!

You may think that only adults can make money.

Well, no! Even if you're young, you can already have some great ideas for making a little pocket money — honestly and smartly.

In our time:

When we were kids, we already knew **how to make honest money**.

In our time, in many neighborhoods, there were blacksmiths. They made pots and kitchen utensils, but often lacked raw materials.

After school and on weekends, we would go looking for **aluminum scraps and old aluminum objects**. We collected them carefully and then sold them to the blacksmiths. The greater the weight, the greater the remuneration.

We also collected **empty bottles**: we washed them carefully with soap, disinfected them, and then sold them at the market. Some of us were more creative, so we used other methods to win honestly.

Thus, very early on, we had learned one essential thing:

Honest work creates value.

But we were missing something even more important. We hadn't learned **how to save, invest, or** make money work for us.

You can do better because today, with this book in your hands, you are better informed than we were at your age.

Observe your surroundings. Seek to understand the needs of your community. Ask questions, then propose useful solutions.

With knowledge, discipline, and creativity, you can go further than our generation.

And maybe, one day, help those who will come after you.

Every era has its challenges.

Yours also has its opportunities.

It's up to you to turn them into the future.

In today's economy, anyone who knows how to sell can make money — even without having money.

You don't need capital to start. You need value.

Offer your selling skills to producers, wholesalers, or retailers. Help them move their products. Generate revenue for them — and you earn a commission in return.

No inventory.

No warehouse.

Small Budget, Big Dreams

No heavy investment.

Just skill, discipline, and consistency.

The income you generate can become your startup capital.

Your service today can finance your business tomorrow.

Selling is not just a job.

It is a gateway to entrepreneurship.

Master the art of sales, and you will never be broke.

 How about starting today?

Why make money young?

Because:

- You learn the value of effort
- You become more responsible
- You can save or invest for your projects
- You don't have to ask all the time anymore!

Simple ideas for children, teenagers

Here are some ideas you can adapt to your age, where you live, and what you like to do:

Activity	What it teaches you

Sell cookies or juices	Organization, hygiene, trade
Make bracelets or drawings	Creativity, patience
Help with shopping	Responsibility, trust
Activity	What it teaches you
Babysitting or helping children	Empathy, autonomy
Create a small journal or blog	Writing, discipline
Resell items you no longer use	Tidying up, negotiation

Example: Amie's Story

Amie loves tales. She had an idea:

She records them with her voice on her phone.

She shares them with other children for 500 GNF per story. In one month, she earned 25,000 GNF!

She used the money to buy a microphone and upgrade her little "studio". She is only 12 years old.

What to always remember

- *Be honest: don't cheat, don't sell what doesn't belong to you.*
- *Be respectful: Ask your parents or an adult for permission.*
- *Be patient: sometimes it works slowly at first, but don't give up!*

Game: Your Mini-Plan

1. What do I like to do? __________

2. Can I do a small activity out of it?
o Yes / No
3. What name could I give to my project? __
4. How much can I earn each week? ______

Write down your plan and talk to a trusted adult. He can help you get started.

To remember:

- You can make money, even if you're young.
- It's not a question of age, but of ideas, respect, and willpower.
- The sooner you start, the faster you become free and confident.

Small challenge: Create your first small project this week. Even if you earn 5,000 GNF, you have started a great path.

CHAPTER 10:
Mistakes to Avoid with Your Money

Chapter 10
Mistakes to Avoid with Your Money

Money is like a seed:

If you take care of it, it grows.

But if you do not, it disappears... very quickly!

In this chapter, you'll learn about the most common mistakes young people (and even adults) make with money — and how to avoid them.

Mistakes to avoid

Mistake # 1*: Spending everything as soon as you receive*

You get 5,000 GNF... and five minutes later, everything is gone into candy or gadgets.

The result? You no longer have anything for your project, your dream, or an important need.

Tip: Apply the 50-30-20 rule

- 50% for your needs
- 30% to treat yourself
- 20% to save

Mistake No. 2: *Buying to impress others*

Do you want the latest bag, the fashionable sneakers, or an expensive item just for others to look at you?

Bad idea! These things do not last and do not make you smarter or freer.

Tip: Ask yourself before each purchase:

"Do I really need it? Or do I just want to please others?"

Mistake No. 3: *Not knowing where your money is going*

Not sure how much you spent this week?

Have you forgotten what your pocket money was used for?

It's like driving without looking at the road!

Tip: Use a small expense book

Records each input (money received) and each output (money spent).

You'll quickly spot waste.

Mistake No. 4: *Thinking you're "too young" to handle money*

"I'm still small, I'll learn later."

Wrong!

The earlier you start, the stronger and freer you'll be later.

Money is like a language: those who learn it early speak better all their lives.

Tip: Talk to your parents about money, read books, and ask questions. It is valuable knowledge.

Mistake No. 5: *Copying Others' Bad Habits*

If you see people always spending, getting into debt, wasting... do not copy them.

Just because "everyone does it" doesn't mean it's good for you.

Tip: Be a positive role model. You can even inspire other children or adults around you!

To remember:

- Managing money means avoiding simple pitfalls.
- Don't spend to impress, but to move forward.
- Be aware of every coin you receive and spend.
- Financial intelligence starts now, not tomorrow.

Small challenge: For a week, write down each expense in a notebook. At the end of the week, analyze:

- What was helpful?
- What was waste?
- What can you change?

Use this page to write down your answers:

CHAPTER 11: Your Budget, Your Superpower!

What is a budget?

Why is this important?

An example of a simple budget

Golden Rules of Good Budget

Chapter 11
Your Budget, Your Superpower!

Imagine that your money is like a football team.

Without a coach, the players run in all directions; with a good plan, they run in the right direction. The team wins!

Your budget is this plan. You choose what each coin or note will do.

With a good budget, you're like a money superhero!

What is a budget?

A budget is simply:

- Know how much you have
- Decide how you're going to use it
- And above all... don't go over what you plan to save.
- You become the conductor of your money.

Why is this important?

- You control your money instead of being subjected to it
- You avoid unnecessary expenses
- You can save more easily
- You prepare for the future with more confidence

An example of a simple budget

Small Budget, Big Dreams

You get 10,000 GNF this week.

You can divide it as follows:

Category	Amount
Savings	2,000 GNF
Useful expenditure	5,000 GNF
Fun / leisure	2,000 GNF
Donate or share	1,000 GNF
Total	10,000 GNF

See? Every franc has its mission!

Make your own budget

1. How much money do you have this week? ____
2. How much do you want to save? ______
3. What are your needs (transport, supplies...)? __
4. What would make you happy? ________
5. Would you like to share a little bit with someone?
   —

Add it all up. If you overshoot, start again until you find the right balance.

Golden Rules of Good Budget

- Be realistic: don't promise more than you can do
- Be disciplined: stick to your plan
- Be flexible: if there is an unforeseen event, adjust without panicking

- Be proud: every week you stay on budget, you gain power

To remember:

- Your budget is your magic tool for managing your money well
- It helps you make smart choices
- It turns your little money into a big project

Small challenge: Take a leaf today. Make your mini budget for the week. Decorate it, stick it on your wall, and try to respect it every day!

CHAPTER 12: Youth Entrepreneurship

Work to learn, not just to win
Mory's story and his first work
The story of Fanta and her iced juice bags

Chapter 12
Youth Entrepreneurship

Work to learn, not just to get paid

Mory's story and his first work

Mory was thirteen years old. He was a curious boy, always ready to help.

During the holidays, he often saw his uncle running a small food shop. One day, he asked him:

"Uncle, can I help you in the shop?"

"Of course," replied the uncle, "but here, you learn before you earn."

Mory thought he would make some quick money. But for the first few days, his uncle gave him nothing.

However, he taught him how to give change, talk to customers, keep a sales book, and monitor stocks.

At first, Mory said to himself:

"Why work if I don't earn anything?"

But as time went on, he realized that he was learning valuable things.

One day, his uncle entrusted him with the cash register and said:

"Today, you're the one responsible. Show me what you've learned. Mory made the sales on his own, counted the money, and finished the day without mistake.

His uncle smiled:

"You see, Mory, now you know how to work seriously. The money will come, but what you have learned will remain for the rest of your life.

The next day, he gave him 20,000 francs and added:

"This is for your work." But remember: real wealth is competence.

On that day, Mory understood an essential lesson:

He who learns before winning, wins twice.

The Story of Hawa and Her Iced Juice Packets

Hawa was twelve years old and lived in a lively neighborhood where the children played football every afternoon.

One day, on her way home from school in the hot sun, she had an idea.

"What if I sold ice cream to children who are playing?"

Her mother gave her her consent, on the condition that she organize herself.

Together they bought a small packet of sachets, sugar, lemons, and flavourings.

Hawa got up early the next day, made the juice, poured it into the bags, and put them in the freezer.

In the afternoon, when the children went out to play, she arrived with her cooler.

"Iced juice!" Very fresh! she cried excitedly.

In a few minutes, she sold everything.

In the evening, she counted her earnings: she had spent 10,000 francs on the ingredients and won 18,000 francs.

Its benefit? 8,000 francs!

Hawa smiled proudly.

The next day, she started again. Then the following week, she offered new flavors.

Very quickly, the whole neighborhood was talking about "the little Hawa of iced juice".

One day, her mistress asked her:

"What do you do with your money, Hawa?"

"I am saving a part to buy a large ice-box," she replied. "Bravo! You're already a small entrepreneur.

Hawa had understood something essential:

Entrepreneurship is not only about selling, but it is also about creating, learning, daring, solving one or more problems, filling a void, or meeting a need.

Financial tip

Always looking to learn something in every experience.

Money is spent, but knowledge will always be useful to you to create it later.

Before you sell something, think about what people really need.

A good entrepreneur is looking to help first, not just to win.

Reflection

Have you ever learned something useful without getting paid?

Maybe help a relative, a friend, or participate in an activity? Every learning is an investment in your future.

What could you sell or create in your school, your neighborhood, or your family?

Maybe a service, an object, or even a useful idea?

Chapter Challenge

1. Find someone around you (a relative, neighbour, or shopkeeper) and offer to help them learn something.

2. Write down what you discover each day.

3. At the end of the week, write down what you've learned—not how much you've earned.

4. Look around you for a little need to satisfy.

5. Offer a simple solution that you could offer or sell.

6. Write down your idea in your notebook and ask an adult for advice.

CHAPTER 13: The First Steps to Your Financial Freedom

Step 1: Change Your Mindset

Step 2: Manage well what you have

Chapter 13: The First Steps to Your Financial Freedom

You got it:

Financial freedom is not just about having a lot of money.

It's having choice, control, and peace in your mind.

The good news is that:

You can start today, even if you're young!

Step 1: Change Your Mindset

It all starts in your head. Tell yourself:

- "I can learn to manage my money."
- "I can become free, no matter where I come from."
- "I can start small, but dream big."

Money is a good servant, but a bad master. Be the one in charge!

Step 2: Manage well what you have

Even if you're just getting 5,000 or 10,000 GNF a week, it's the perfect workout.

- Make a budget
- Write down your expenses
- Save a little, even 500 GNF
- Think before you buy

Whoever manages small amounts well will be ready to manage large sums.

Step 3: Learn continuously

Every month, discover something new:

- How do banks work?
- What is insurance?
- How do I save for a project?
- What is a savings account?
- How do I start a business?

Read, watch videos, ask questions.

Financial education is your real asset!

Step 4: Start a small project

You don't need millions to get started.

Here are some simple ideas:

- Sell homemade cookies
- Help other people sell their products
- Create bracelets or jewelry
- Organize a raffle or educational game
- Write tales, poems etc.
- Helping someone with their homework for a small contribution

The goal is not to get rich right away, but to understand the value of money and create income.

Step 5: Avoid Pitfalls

- Don't spend money to impress others
- Don't blindly copy what others are doing
- Don't believe in "easy and quick wins"
- Don't be discouraged if it doesn't work out the first time

Be patient, honest, and disciplined. This is the real wealth.

To remember:

- Financial freedom starts in your head
- It is built with small steps, every day
- You're never too young to start with

Small challenge: Write down a small financial goal (e.g., save 10,000 GNF in 1 month or sell 5 simple products).

Share it with someone who supports you and start today!

OVERALL CONCLUSION

Overall Conclusion

Money doesn't buy happiness, but it can build your future.

Dear reader,

You've just been on an important trip.

A journey into the world of money, but also into the world of ideas, dreams, and responsibilities.

You have learned that:

- Money is a tool, not an end
- Being rich is not only about having millions, but about understanding, managing, and making work of what you have.
- You can become an opportunity creator, even with little
- True wealth is also knowledge, discipline, generosity, and freedom

A message for you, the child or teenager.

You're not too young to understand money.

You're not too small to do big things.

You're not too poor to dream of financial freedom.

Small Budget, Big Dreams

Every coin you save, every idea you test, every mistake you turn into a lesson... It's a brick in the bridge of your future.

In short, you don't have to be born rich.

You need to understand the rules of the game, start small, and believe that you can make a difference.

You can become a builder of freedom, an example for your generation, a silent hero in your family.

And it all starts today.

Not with millions.

But with a decision and ideas.

Learn.

Take action. Share.

A message for parents, uncles, aunts, and educators.

By talking about money with our children, we give them much more than a lesson:

We give them a chance to choose their lives,

We avoid the traps of over-indebtedness, dependence, and ignorance,

We give them the power to say no to poverty, yes to responsible ambition.

You have a vital role to play in your children's understanding of money and the **noble value of honest work.**

From an early age, you can teach them that money doesn't fall from the sky: it has to be **earned**, it has to be **earned**, and above all, it is **managed** wisely.

Give them small responsibilities at home, such as taking out the garbage, washing vehicles, cleaning, tidying up, helping with home organization, or doing other household chores appropriate for their age. Even if your standard of living is high, avoid having everything done for you, including by domestic servants.

The objective is not constrained, but **learning to make an effort and take responsibility**.

For each task completed, **pay them financially**, either weekly or monthly. Then establish a simple yet powerful habit: smartly sharing **their earnings**.

Give them separate envelopes (or boxes) and teach them how to divide their money:

- **Savings**: to learn patience and foresight
- **Personal expenses**: to manage their desires with discipline
- **Donations/sharing**: to cultivate generosity
- **Investing**: to understand how money can work

When the child wants to buy something, invite them to **open their savings envelope first**. Set clear rules together: those who save more will be rewarded for their efforts. For example, you can decide to add a fixed amount to top up their savings — a concrete way to show them that **discipline pays off**.

Each month, you can also discreetly slip a small bonus into the investment envelope, without telling them. After a year, open this envelope **together**. Compare what they put in and what the money produced **without extra effort**.

This will then be the ideal time to explain to them:

- **the** power of investment,

- passive **income**,

- and this fascinating idea that you can make money even while you sleep.

Help them understand this fundamental truth:

Every franc in your hands can become an employee. All you have to do is give it a mission.

By passing on these habits to them today, you are giving them much more than money: you are giving them a **compass for life**.

Financial education is a key to the future.

Let's pass it on simply, early, and with love.

Final Words

Your future is like a garden: if you plant good seeds today, you will reap beautiful fruits tomorrow.

You discovered in this book that money is not a mystery reserved for adults or the rich. It is a tool. And if you learn to use it intelligently, it can help you achieve even the biggest dreams.

Remember this:

- Start small, but start well.
- Learn how to manage before you try to win.
- Your habits today shape your freedom tomorrow.

Even with a small budget, your dreams can become big if you accompany them with discipline, patience, and courage.

So, don't be afraid to start. Every step counts. And remember: *the greatest wealth is to learn and believe in yourself.*

*"**Money doesn't buy happiness, but good financial education can save you a lot of misfortune**."* So, choose to be free, curious, creative, and responsible.

The future is not to be waited for... it has to be built.

And you can.

75

APPENDICES

Some quotes from the author that encourage reflection
Some examples of Pedagogical Sheets

A few thought-provoking quotes

On small steps

"Great successes are always born from small steps repeated with consistency. Manage your small budget well today, and tomorrow your dreams will come true. »

— *Abdoulaye Amie Soumah, MBA*

On freedom

"Financial freedom is not an unattainable dream. It begins with knowledge, is built with discipline, and is accomplished with perseverance. »

— *Abdoulaye Amie Soumah, MBA*

On youth and the future

"Every child who learns to manage a small budget becomes an adult who can build a great future."

— *Abdoulaye Amie Soumah, MBA*

"True wealth does not begin in your wallet, but in your mind. If you change your way of thinking, you will change the way you live. »

— *Abdoulaye Amie Soumah, MBA*

LIST OF PROPOSED EDUCATIONAL SHEETS

List of proposed educational sheets

1.   Origin, barter → currency → credit card

2.   **Needs and Wants**

Classify and discuss what is essential vs. what is optional.

3. Make a Budget

Activity: Divide 100 fictitious units between food, transport, leisure, and savings.

Exercise: compare two budgets (one balanced, one unbalanced).

4. Assets and Liabilities

Game: images/objects to be classified (e.g., rented house, luxury car, computer to work on, etc.).

Discussion: what brings in money, what makes money go out.

5. Active vs. Passive Income

Tell two short stories (example: one child sells candy every day = active income / another creates a small booklet that he resells several times = passive income).

Exercise: Identify the difference.

6. Savings and Goals

Activity: drawing a dream (toy, bike, travel).

Calculate how much you need to save per week to get it.

7. The Power of Small Amounts (Money Habits)

Example: save 100 GNF per day → how much at the end of the month/year?

A set of simple calculations to show growth.

8. Introduction to the Stock Market (Simple Level)

Role-play: each group represents a company, and the others buy/sell "shares".

Discussion: why the value can go up or down.

9. The Difference Between Expense and Investment
Activity: comparing "buying candy" vs "buying a book".

Guided discussion: Which one pays tomorrow?

10. The Importance of Generosity and Sharing

Thought: What would you do if you had 10000 GNF more?

Introduce the notion of donation, solidarity, and social impact.

11. My First Personal Financial Plan

Exercise: each student makes a small sheet with:

1   priority needs
2   A savings goal
3   An idea for future investment

SOME EXAMPLES OFEDUCATIONAL SHEETS

<u>**Advice for parents**</u>: learning about money through everyday life

Objective

To help parents instill in their children, from an early age, a **healthy understanding of money, honest work, saving, investing,** and **sharing**.

The role of parents

Parents are their children's **primary financial educators**. It is at home that the child learns:

- that money is **earned**,
- that he **manages** himself,
- and that it must be used responsibly **and wisely**.

1. Learn the value of honest work

Give your children **small**, age-appropriate household responsibilities, such as:

o take out the garbage,

o washing vehicles,

o tidying up and cleaning the house,

o help organize the home.

Even if your standard of living is high, avoid having everything done for them, including by servants.

The objective is to teach them that **effort precedes reward**.

2. Reward the effort

Pay children for tasks performed by:

- weekly or
- monthly,

according to clear and consistent rules. This allows them to understand that **work creates value**.

3. The envelope (or box) method

Teach your kids how to divide their earnings into **four envelopes**:

1. **Saving** – to learn patience and foresight
2. **Personal expenses** – to manage their desires
3. **Donations / Sharing** – to cultivate generosity
4. **Investing** – to find out how money can work

When a child wants to buy something, first ask them to open their **savings envelope**.

4. Reward discipline

Set simple rules:

- those who **save more** earn more,
- You can add a **fixed bonus** to savings to encourage discipline.

Each month, you can also discreetly slip a small amount into the **Investment envelope**, without telling the child.

5. Understanding Investing and Passive Income

After several months (or a year), open **the Investment envelope** together. Compare:

- what the child has put on,
- and what money has been able to produce.

This is the perfect time to explain:

the power of investment,

passive **income**,

the idea that money can work **even when you sleep**.

Key message to convey to the child

Every franc in your hands can become an employee.
All you have to do is give it a mission.

By teaching these simple habits, you are giving your children much more than money: you are giving them a **compass for life**, based on work, discipline, generosity, and freedom.

Pedagogical sheet 1
What is money?

Learning Objectives: Understand the origin and role of money

- Origin, barter $\rightarrow$ money $\rightarrow$ bank card
- Discover the evolution of barter towards money-
Know why money facilitates exchanges.

Course schedule: 1 Introduction (10 min):

Discussion of bartering (e.g., giving a fish for rice).2. Activity (20 min):

Compare barter and currency with simple examples.3. Exercise (10 min):

Each student imagines a barter situation and transforms it into an exchange for money. 4. Conclusion (5 min): Money simplifies life because it is accepted by all.

Evaluation:

Ask students to give a concrete example of bartering, then of a monetary transaction.

Pedagogical sheet 2
Needs and Wants

Level: Students from 8 to 12 years old

Duration: 45 minutes

Learning Objectives

- Understand the difference between a need and a want.
- Be able to classify concrete examples.
- Thinking about your own consumption choices.

Material

- Blackboard / chalk or projector
- Sheets with pictures or words (rice, toy, shoes, candy, medicine, bicycle, ice cream, notebooks, phone, etc.)
- Workbook or worksheet for each student

Course schedule

1. Introduction (10 min)

    - Ask the question: "If you had 10,000 Francs today, what would you do with it?"
    - Listen to some answers, then introduce the two categories:

Need = what is essential to live and learn well (food, housing, notebooks, etc.).

o Craving = what is pleasant but not vital (candy, video games, designer clothes...).

2. Main activity (20 min)

- Distribute the cards with pictures/words.
- As a group, students must glue or place each card in the correct column: Needs or Wants.
- Group discussion: Some objects can be in both categories depending on the context (e.g., a bicycle may be a need if it is the only way to get to school).

3. Individual exercise (10 min)

- Each student records 3 needs and 3 personal desires in their notebook.
- Reflection question: "If you could only pay for one thing, which one would you choose and why?"

4. Conclusion & Moral (5 min)

- Remember that knowing how to distinguish between needs and wants helps to better manage your money.
- Give a small challenge: "This week, before you buy something, always ask yourself: is this a need or a want?"

Assessment

- Observation of participation in the ranking game.
- Verification of written exercises.

- Ability to explain the need/want difference in their own words.

87

Pedagogical sheet 3
Make a Budget

Level: Students from 9 to 14 years old

Duration: 45 minutes

Learning Objectives

- Understand what a budget is.
- Learn how to divide a sum of money between different needs.
- Identify the importance of balancing spending, saving, and leisure.

Material

- Blackboard / chalk or projector
- Worksheets with an empty budget table
- Fictitious banknotes (paper or tokens) representing the money to be managed

Course schedule

1. Introduction (10 min)

   - Ask the question: "What would you do if you were given two hundred thousand dollars today?"
   - Explain: A budget is a plan that tells you how to use your money in a balanced way.

2. Main activity (20 min)

- Give each group a fictitious sum of 100 units (in tokens or paper).

- Present 4 categories:
  o Food & Essential Needs
  o Transport & école
  o Hobbies (cinema, games, clothes)
  o Savings & future plans
- Each group must divide the 100 units into these categories.

3. Individual exercise (10 min)

- Each student fills in a small budget table with 50 fictitious units.
- Question: "If you want to keep 10 for savings, how much is left for the other categories?"

4. Conclusion & Moral (5 min)

- A budget is about controlling your money rather than letting it control you.
- Even small amounts deserve a budget.

Assessment

- Check if students know how to balance a budget.
- Observe the choices made: do they understand that savings are as important as immediate needs?

Pedagogical sheet 4
Assets and Liabilities

Level: Students from 9 to 14 years old

Duration: 45 minutes

Learning Objectives

• Understand the difference between assets and liabilities.
• Identify, with simple examples, what brings in money and what takes it out.
• Develop the reflex to seek to own more assets than liabilities.

Material

• Sheets with two columns: Assets and Liabilities
• Images or cards representing objects (house, bike, toy, shop, book, smartphone, etc.)

Course schedule

1. Introduction (10 min)

• Question to students:

"Do all the objects we own help us make money?"

• Explain simply:

o   Assets = things that put money in your pocket.

o   Liabilities = things that take money out of your pocket.

2.   Hands-on activity (20 min)

- Distribute cards representing objects:
  o   Examples of assets: a cornfield, a book that is being resold, a small shop, a juice machine.
  o   Examples of liabilities: a motorcycle that needs to be constantly repaired, a very expensive phone, and luxury clothes.
- In groups, students must classify the cards in the correct column.

3.   Individual exercise (10 min)

- Each student writes 2 examples of assets and 2 examples of passives in their own life or environment.

4.   Conclusion & Moral (5 min)

- An asset works for you.
- A Liability makes you work for it.
- The key to wealth is to accumulate assets and limit liabilities.

Assessment

- Check whether the students have correctly classified the objects.
- Ask the question: "If you receive 20,000 GNF, would you rather buy a toy (liability) or a book that you can lend for a small (asset) gain?"

Pedagogical sheet 5
Savings and Investment

Level: Students from 9 to 14 years old

Duration: 45 minutes

Learning Objectives

- Understand the difference between saving and investing.
- Know why it's important to set money aside.
- Discover simple examples of investing accessible to children and families.

Material

- A box or piggy bank (to illustrate savings).
- Images of objects or projects (notebook, bike, shop, field, juice machine).
- Table or sheet with two columns: Savings and Investment.

Course schedule

1. Introduction (10 min)

- Ask the question:

"If you receive 20,000 GNF today, what do you do? Do you spend it all or keep some of it? »

- Explain:
  - Saving = saving some of your money for later.

  - Investing = using your money to make it even more money.

2. Hands-on activity (20 min)

- Show a piggy bank and explain that it's a good habit to start saving.
- Then give simple examples of investment:
  - Buy a sheep that will give birth.
  - Planting corn to resell. o Buy a book that teaches you a skill to win later.
- Have students sort cards in the Savings or Investment columns.

3. Individual exercise (10 min)

- Each student writes:
  - Something they would like to save for (e.g. a new notebook, a ball). o An idea for an investment that he could make with 30,000 GNF (e.g., sell juice, raise chickens).

4. Conclusion & Moral (5 min)

- Savings protect against the unexpected.
- Investing makes your money grow.
- To move towards financial freedom:
  - Save first, invest later.

Assessment

- Check whether students can give concrete examples of savings and investment.
- Final question:

"If you receive 50,000 GNF, how much do you keep, and how could you make it grow?"

Notes for educators

The educational sheets presented in the appendix to this book are not intended to be exhaustive or prescriptive. They are, above all, **examples of guidelines and pedagogical avenues**, proposed for information purposes.

Teachers, educators, and trainers remain **entirely free** to adapt, enrich, or replace these approaches according to their context, their audience, and the methods they consider most effective.

The main objective is to facilitate the transmission of key financial education messages with clarity, creativity, **and ease**, while respecting the pedagogical freedom of each individual.

ABOUT THE AUTHOR

Abdoulaye Amie Soumah, MBA, is a visionary author, investor, and technology professional, deeply committed to transforming minds and elevating individuals. Passionate about financial education, personal development, and social innovation, he dedicates his energy to imparting knowledge that liberates, inspires, and paves the way for a better future.

Author of *Forged* Destiny and *Fear Overcome*, he shares a strong conviction in his books:

Freedom begins in the mind, long before it appears in life.

Through his writings, he highlights the power of resilience, the strength of inner courage, and the need to overcome the fears that hold back so many talents—the fear of public speaking, the fear of entrepreneurship, the fear of failure.

With *Small Budget, Big Dreams*, he pursues his mission: to provide children, families, and educators with simple, clear, and accessible tools to lay the foundations for healthy, liberating financial thinking from a young age because he believes that every child, wherever he or she is born, deserves to grow up with the keys to success.

With an engineering degree in **Bridges and Roads** from the Gamal Abdel Nasser University in Conakry, a BA in **Telecommunications and Network Management** from *the New York Institute of Technology* (United States), and an **MBA** from *the Keller Graduate School of Management* (United States), he combines a high-level education with a rich and diversified professional experience.

Born in Conakry and now based in the United States, married and father of three children, he remains deeply attached to his Guinean roots. He is actively involved in educational and entrepreneurial initiatives aimed at creating a lasting impact, uncovering talent, and fostering a confident, free, and responsible generation.

Helping everyone express their best selves is not a choice for him; it is a life mission.

Remember this simple truth: "Great dreams are not built with big money, but with small decisions made wisely over time."

www.ingramcontent.com/pod-product-compliance
Lightning Source LLC
Chambersburg PA
CBHW071350150726
47997CB00002B/925